## Hello, Family Members,

Learning to read is one of the most important accomplishments of early childhood. **Hello Reader!** books are designed to help children become skilled readers who like to read. Beginning readers learn to read by remembering frequently used words like "the," "is," and "and"; by using phonics skills to decode new words; and by interpreting picture and text clues. These books provide both the stories children enjoy and the structure they need to read fluently and independently. Here are suggestions for helping your child *before*, *during*, and *after* reading:

### Before

- Look at the cover and pictures and have your child predict what the story is about.
- Read the story to your child.
- Encourage your child to chime in with familiar words and phrases.
- Echo read with your child by reading a line first and having your child read it after you do.

### During

- Have your child think about a word he or she does not recognize right away. Provide hints such as "Let's see if we know the sounds" and "Have we read other words like this one?"
- Encourage your child to use phonics skills to sound out new words.
- Provide the word for your child when more assistance is needed so that he or she does not struggle and the experience of reading with you is a positive one.
- Encourage your child to have fun by reading with a lot of expression . . . like an actor!

### After

- Have your child keep lists of interesting and favorite words.
- Encourage your child to read the books over and over again. Have him or her read to brothers, sisters, grandparents, and even teddy bears. Repeated readings develop confidence in young readers.
- Talk about the stories. Ask and answer questions. Share ideas about the funniest and most interesting characters and events in the stories.

I do hope that you and your child enjoy this book.

—Francie Alexander
   Reading Specialist,
   Scholastic's Learning Ventures

*For Danicka, who's blessed with a teacher's heart.*
*— S.W.B.*

*To Lila Higgins*
*— T.M.*

ISBN: 0-439-20641-3

Text copyright © 2000 by Sonia W. Black.
Illustrations copyright © 2000 by Turi MacCombie.
All rights reserved. Published by Scholastic Inc.
SCHOLASTIC, HELLO READER, CARTWHEEL BOOKS
and associated logos are trademarks and/or registered trademarks of Scholastic Inc.

Library of Congress Cataloging-in-Publication Data available

30 29 28 27 26 25 24 23 22                         8 9 10 11 12 13/0

Printed in the U.S.A.   23
First printing, December 2000

# Follow
## the
# Polar Bears

by Sonia W. Black

Illustrated by Turi MacCombie

## Hello Reader! Science—Level 1

SCHOLASTIC INC. Cartwheel B·O·O·K·S ®

New York  Toronto  London  Auckland  Sydney
Mexico City  New Delhi  Hong Kong

Polar bears here.
Polar bears there.
Come! Let's follow
the polar bears.

Polar bear is snug
inside her den.
No food. No friends.
Waiting.
    Waiting.
        Waiting.

Then—
finally, her waiting ends.

Here comes one cub.
Here comes another.
Polar bear twins,
a sister and a brother!

Mother bear cuddles
her babies soft as silk.
Cubs huddle and nurse
on Mom's warm milk.

One week, two weeks,
three weeks go past.
Four, five, six weeks . . .
their eyes open at last!

By seven or eight weeks,
or maybe one more,
the cubs stand up
and walk on all fours.

Ready, set . . .
they go outdoors.
There's so much to learn,
so much to explore.

Little cubs, look —
Ooh! What a sight!
Ice is everywhere.
Everything's snow-white.

*Sniff! Sniff! Sniff!*
Smell the danger in the air.
Ice foxes are very near.
Little cubs, BEWARE!

*Brrr!*
Freezing winds blow,
but no need to worry.
Cubs stay warm
in their coats
thick and furry.

Whoops! Be careful!
Don't tumble! Don't slip!
Pads on their feet
help give a firm grip.

Cubs roll.

Cubs run.

Cubs swim
and have fun!

Hungry cubs watch as
Mom hunts for meals.
Her long, sharp claws
catch slippery seals.

Polar bears' teeth
tear, rip, and chew
walruses and salmon,
birds and seaweed, too!

Once small cubs,
now they're all grown.
It's time to go off
and live on their own.

Polar bears, polar bears.
Each finds a mate.
Soon—there's something
to celebrate. . . .

Polar bears here.
Polar bears there.
New polar bear cubs are
EVERYWHERE!